SPORTS STARS

HAKEEM OLAJUWON

THE DREAM

By Miles Harvey

CHILDREN'S PRESS
A Division of Grolier Publishing
Sherman Turnpike
Danbury, Connecticut 06816

Photo Credits

Cover, 5, Focus on Sports; 6, ©Barry Gossage Photography; 9, ©Jason Lauré; 11, Tim DeFrisco/©Allsport; 12, UPI/Bettmann; 14, Focus on Sports; 16, 19, UPI/Bettmann; 20, Focus on Sports; 22, 25, 27, 28, 30, UPI/Bettmann; 33, 34, AP/Wide World; 37, ©Scott Wachter/Sports Photo Masters, Inc.; 38, ©Brian Drake/Sportschrome; 41, AP/Wide World; 43, ©Noren Troten/ Sports Photo Masters, Inc.

Project Editors: Shari Joffe and Mark Friedman
Design: Beth Herman Design Associates
Photo Editor: Jan Izzo

Library of Congress Cataloging-in-Publication Data

Harvey, Miles.
Hakeem Olajuwon: the dream / by Miles Harvey.
p. cm. – (Sports stars)
ISBN 0-516-04387-0
1. Olajuwon, Hakeem, 1963- –Juvenile literature. 2. Basketball players–United States–Biography–Juvenile literature. [1. Olajuwon, Hakeem, 1963-. 2. Basketball players. 3. Blacks–Nigeria–Biography.] I. Title. II. Series.
GV884.043H37 1994
796.323'092–dc20
[B] 94-14400
CIP
AC

Printed in the United States of America.
4 5 6 7 8 9 10 R 03 02 01 00 99 98 97 96

HAKEEM OLAJUWON

THE DREAM

Rockets

☆ ☆ ☆

Hakeem Olajuwon isn't the most famous player in pro basketball. But he may be the best.

He can score like Shaquille O'Neal. He can block shots and rebound like David Robinson. He can make passes and steals like Scottie Pippen.

"He's unstoppable, the best player in the league," says an executive for one NBA team. Adds one of Olajuwon's teammates on the Houston Rockets: "We've got the best player in the NBA playing on our team in Hakeem. It's unbelievable how good he is."

Hakeem takes such praise in stride. "I never felt like I was better than any of the other players," he says. "But I also never felt like anyone else was better than me."

☆ ☆ ☆

Hakeem's life story is as amazing as one of his monster slam dunks. He was born on January 21, 1963, in Nigeria, a country in the western part of Africa. Many African Americans have ancestors who came from this region hundreds of years ago as slaves. The African traditions these slaves brought with them have become an important part of American life. For example, jazz, rock, and hip-hop music can all be traced back to the music that the slaves brought over from West Africa.

Today, Nigeria has more people than any other country in Africa. It is as big as the states of California, Arizona, and New Mexico combined. In some parts of Nigeria, elephants, giraffes, and lions roam the countryside. But Hakeem comes from Lagos, which is Nigeria's largest city.

"People think all of Africa is the jungle because that's what they see on TV," explains Hakeem. "But Lagos is just like New York—crowded."

A bustling street in Lagos, Nigeria, Hakeem's home city

☆ ☆ ☆

A hundred languages are spoken in Nigeria. That's because more than 200 different ethnic groups live there, and each group has its own customs and history. Hakeem's family is part of a group of people known as the Yoruba. In the Yoruban language, Olajuwon means "always being on top."

But when it comes to basketball, Hakeem hasn't always been at the top. Basketball isn't very popular in Nigeria—so Hakeem didn't even play the sport when he was a little boy. Instead, he and his four brothers and one sister learned such sports as field hockey and track. Hakeem loved to play handball. He also became an excellent soccer goalie.

OLAJUWON
34

Hakeem started playing basketball late in his childhood, but he learned the game quickly.

☆ ☆ ☆

But Hakeem didn't look like a lot of other soccer players. That's because by the time Hakeem was 16 years old, he stood almost seven feet tall. One day, the basketball coach at his school asked Hakeem if he was interested in being on the basketball team. Hakeem said he didn't really know how to play, but was willing to give it a try.

Hakeem was a quick learner. Some of his skills as a soccer goalie helped him make the adjustment to basketball. For instance, Hakeem discovered that blocking shots in basketball requires some of the same instincts as stopping shots on goal in soccer.

By the time he was 17, Hakeem was playing on Nigeria's national team in the 1980 Junior All-Africa Games. That same year, Hakeem came to the United States for the first time. He was thinking about attending college there.

It took a while before University of Houston coach Guy Lewis (right) was convinced that Hakeem could play college ball.

☆ ☆ ☆

At first, Hakeem didn't like America. He was used to Nigeria's warm climate, and it was chilly outside when Hakeem's plane landed in New York City. "I thought it was too cold for me to live in this country," Hakeem remembers.

Hakeem soon went to Texas to visit the University of Houston. The weather there, Hakeem discovered, was much milder. The university's basketball coach, Guy Lewis, had heard that Hakeem was good. But Lewis doubted that the Nigerian teenager could compete with American players.

HOUSTON
34
CHARLES
43

☆ ☆ ☆

"I've had hundreds of foreign kids referred to us over the years," Lewis later recalled. "Frankly, they just don't play basketball in most countries the way they play it in the United States." But after watching Hakeem on the court, Lewis was impressed. He could see that Hakeem had a lot to learn about basketball. But the coach thought that if Hakeem practiced hard, he could become a star someday. Lewis offered Hakeem a scholarship to play basketball for the Cougars.

☆ ☆ ☆

In January of 1981, Hakeem enrolled at the university. He had been playing basketball for only a couple of years—and his inexperience showed. “I don’t care how you slice it, he flat-out didn’t know how to play,” the coach later explained. Hakeem wasn’t allowed to be on the team during his first months at the school. That frustrated him. He was also homesick. He missed his father, Salaam, and his mother, Abike. He also missed Nigerian food, such as a meal called *fufu* and a fried banana treat called *dodos*. On top of all that, Hakeem’s teammates and classmates sometimes teased him about his African accent and customs. “That [was] not funny to me,” he says.

But Hakeem stayed in school and kept practicing. He was determined to be a great player. “Everything that is good is the result of hard work and commitment,” says Hakeem.

In college, Hakeem became known for his spectacular dunks.

Originally known as "Akeem" in America, Hakeem later changed his name—"Hakeem" is a more accurate translation in English.

☆ ☆ ☆

Hakeem got better and better. By the beginning of the 1981-82 season, he was ready to help the Cougars. The University of Houston had some of the best college players in the country that year, including future NBA All-Star Clyde Drexler. With Hakeem on the Cougars, the team became even better.

The Cougars had a great season. They almost made it to the national championship game. But they lost to the University of North Carolina, led by Michael Jordan, in the semifinal game. Michael's team went on to win the championship that year.

After the season, Hakeem continued to work hard on his basketball skills. He was pretty good, but he wasn't great yet. He hoped that if he improved enough, the Cougars could win the championship the following year.

Hakeem yanks down one of his 18 rebounds against North Carolina State in the 1983 NCAA championship game.

☆ ☆ ☆

In the 1982-83 season, Hakeem started to demonstrate his true talent. Fans were calling him "The Dream" because he was becoming such a good player. The Cougars had a great year, winning 31 games and losing only 3 in the regular season.

In the post-season championship tournament, Hakeem was fantastic. He had 21 points, 6 rebounds, and 2 blocked shots against Memphis State, followed by 20 points, 13 rebounds, and 8 blocks against Villanova. In the semi-final game, he had 21 points, 22 rebounds, and 8 blocks, as the Cougars beat Louisville to make it to the championship game.

Houston's opponent was North Carolina State. The showdown proved to be one of the greatest games in college basketball history. Hakeem gave an awesome performance—scoring 20 points, grabbing 18 rebounds, and swatting away 7 shots. But despite his efforts, North Carolina State won the game 54-52 on a basket in the final seconds.

☆ ☆ ☆

Hakeem was sad that his team didn't win the championship, but he could be proud of his own accomplishments. After the final game was over, Hakeem was named the Most Valuable Player in the tournament. It was the first time in 17 years that the MVP award was given to a player from the team that had lost.

Hakeem improved even more in 1983-84. He was the nation's leading college player in shooting percentage and in rebounding. His team also did well. For the second season in a row, the Cougars made it all the way to the national championship game.

This time, they played the Georgetown Hoyas, led by 7-foot-tall Patrick Ewing. Patrick and Hakeem were considered the best two centers in college basketball, and fans all over the country were excited to see the two play against each other. In the big game, Olajuwon performed better than Ewing. But Patrick's team won the championship by a score of 84-75.

Hakeem gets in Patrick Ewing's face to block a shot in the 1984 NCAA championship game.

☆ ☆ ☆

Hakeem ended his college career after the 1983-84 season. In just three years, he had gone from being an awkward teenager to being one of the best college players in the United States. Hakeem was so good, in fact, that sports reporters and coaches voted him the Southwest Conference Player of the Decade. Now it was time for Hakeem to try professional basketball. The NBA's Houston Rockets had the first pick in the 1984 college draft. That meant that the Rockets could get the best college player in the country for their team.

The Rockets had an opportunity to select the amazing Michael Jordan from the University of North Carolina. But they thought that Hakeem could help their team even more than Michael. So the Rockets selected Hakeem with their number-one pick. The Chicago Bulls ended up getting Jordan on the third pick of the draft.

Hakeem shows off his new jersey after the Houston Rockets made him the first pick in the 1984 NBA draft.

The next season, the Twin Towers led the Rockets all the way to the NBA championship series. But the mighty Boston Celtics, led by Larry Bird, defeated Houston four games to two.

A lot of people thought Hakeem and the Rockets would get another shot at the championship very soon. But the team wasn't able to live up to people's expectations. The Rockets weren't terrible, but they weren't great, either. Between the 1986-87 season and the 1990-91 season, the Rockets made the playoffs every year. But they were always quickly eliminated. Houston even traded Ralph Sampson in an effort to improve. But the trade didn't really help.

Hakeem fought hard, but the Rockets were beaten by Larry Bird and the Boston Celtics in the 1986 NBA Championship Series.

HOUSTON
34
NDERSON
15
33

☆ ☆ ☆

Even though his team struggled, Hakeem played great. He was selected to the NBA All-Star team in each of his first six seasons in the league. In each year during that stretch, he averaged more than 20 points and 10 rebounds per game. He was named to the All-NBA first team in 1987, 1988, and 1989; and the All-NBA second team in 1986 and 1990. In 1989, he became the first player in NBA history to have more than 200 blocks and 200 steals in the same season. In the 1990 season, he became the second player ever to grab 1,000 rebounds and block 300 shots in the same year.

Yet despite all his individual success, Hakeem wasn't happy. "To me, what is important is who has the best team," he explains. And Hakeem's team was far from being the best.

☆ ☆ ☆

The 1991-92 season was especially frustrating for Hakeem. The Rockets lost four of the final five games and missed the playoffs for the first time since Hakeem had joined the team. Off the court, Hakeem got into arguments with the team's owner. Some people thought that the Rockets would trade Hakeem.

But Hakeem stayed in Houston. And the next season, things began to get better. With the help of their new coach, Rudy Tomjanovich, the Rockets won 41 out of their last 50 regular-season games. The Rockets made it to the Western Conference semifinals before the Seattle Supersonics eliminated them in a close, seven-game series.

34

34
21

☆ ☆ ☆

It had been an incredible year for Hakeem. On offense, he averaged 26.1 points per game—his best season ever. On defense, he led the NBA in blocked shots and was named the NBA Defensive Player of the Year. He finished second to Charles Barkley for the NBA Most Valuable Player award.

But one of Hakeem's biggest achievements in 1993 took place off the basketball court. In April, he became a United States citizen. "It's a great source of pride," he explains. "This country has been very good to me and I wanted to be a real part of it. Now I can vote."

The next season, Hakeem and the Rockets got off to an amazing start. They won their first 15 games. That winning streak tied a 45-year-old NBA record for the best start to a season.

☆ ☆ ☆

Hakeem and the Rockets finished the year as well as they had started it. They wound up the regular season with 58 wins and 24 losses, second best in the Western Conference. Hakeem was named the NBA Most Valuable Player. Hakeem was proud of the award, but he had his mind on an NBA championship. "A championship is team glory, where the MVP is an individual honor. You always take the team first."

And Hakeem's team found glory. They made it all the way to the NBA Finals, where they defeated the New York Knicks. The Rockets fell behind in the series, but they came back to win the last two games at home. In Game Six, Hakeem played brilliantly, blocking a Knicks' shot at the buzzer to save a thrilling 86–84 win. And in Game Seven, Hakeem's 25 points and 10 rebounds led the way. The Rockets beat the Knicks 90–84, and the city of Houston had its first champion in a major sport.

Hakeem went up against Patrick Ewing in the 1994 NBA Finals, and the Rockets won the title in seven thrilling games.

☆ ☆ ☆

After the game, Hakeem was named Most Valuable Player for the Finals. It was a rare double honor for a player to win MVP awards in both the regular season and the playoffs. Hakeem said, "If you wrote a book, it couldn't come out any better, for this series, for this season. I'm so happy."

And for Hakeem the Dream, the glory continued a year later. In the 1994-95 regular season, Hakeem suffered from injuries and illness, and the Rockets seemed likely to lose their championship. But Hakeem came alive in the playoffs. In the NBA Finals, he dominated the Orlando Magic and their superstar center, Shaquille O'Neal. The Rockets swept the Magic 4–0 for their second consecutive championship.

Hakeem was at the height of his career, and he still dreamed of more championships.

NFL

Chronology

1963 – Hakeem Olajuwon is born on January 21, in Lagos, Nigeria. Hakeem's father, Salaam, and mother, Abike, own a cement business in the city.

1979 – Hakeem plays in his first organized basketball game.

1980 – Hakeem plays on Nigeria's national team in the Junior All-Africa Games.

– Hakeem comes to the United States for the first time. He is offered a basketball scholarship by the University of Houston.

1981 – Hakeem begins classes at the university in January, and starts playing for the Cougars in the fall.

1982 – The University of Houston makes it to the NCAA semifinals before being defeated by the University of North Carolina, led by Michael Jordan. North Carolina ends up winning the tournament.

1983 – The Cougars make it all the way to the NCAA championship game before being defeated 54-52 by North Carolina State. Hakeem is named Most Valuable Player of the tournament.

☆ ☆ ☆

1984 – Hakeem leads the nation's college players in shooting percentage and rebounding. He becomes only the third player in major-college basketball to lead the nation in at least two categories.

– The Cougars again make it to the NCAA tournament final, this time losing to Georgetown, 84-75. The Cougars finish with an 88-16 record for Hakeem's three seasons with the team.

– The Houston Rockets select Hakeem with the first pick of the National Basketball Association's college draft.

1985 – Hakeem is selected to the first team of the NBA All-Rookie squad and is chosen to be on the All-Star team. He finishes second to Jordan in the Rookie of the Year vote. Hakeem is voted second team All-Defense. He finishes fourth in the league in rebounding and second in blocked shots.

1986 – The Rockets make the NBA Finals, where they are defeated by the Boston Celtics four games to two.

– Hakeem again makes the All-Star team. He finishes eighth in the league in scoring, third in blocked shots, and eleventh in steals.

1987 – Hakeem is chosen to be on the first team of the All-NBA and All-NBA defense squads. He starts the All-Star game for the Western Conference.

☆ ☆ ☆

1988 – Hakeem is again named to the first team of the All-NBA and All-NBA defense squads. Again, he starts in the All-Star game.

1989 – Hakeem is on the first team of the All-NBA squad for the third straight year.
– Hakeem again starts the All-Star game. He leads the NBA in rebounding, and becomes the first player in NBA history to record 200 blocked shots and 200 steals in the same season.

1990 – On March 29 against Milwaukee, Hakeem records a "quadruple double." That means he got more than ten points, rebounds, assists, and blocked shots.
– Hakeem becomes only the fourth player in league history to lead the NBA in rebounding for two consecutive seasons. He leads the league in blocked shots, with 376. He becomes the second player in NBA history to have more than 1,000 rebounds and 300 blocks in the same season.

1991 – On January 3, Chicago's Bill Cartright elbows Hakeem in the face, breaking bones around Hakeem's eye. Hakeem misses 25 games due to the injury.
– Hakeem leads the league in blocked shots for the second straight year.

☆ ☆ ☆

1992 – The Rockets briefly suspend Hakeem for missing games. He claims that he can't play in the games because he's injured.

1993 – Hakeem is named the NBA's Defensive Player of the Year, makes the All-Star team for the eighth time, and is named to the first team of the All-NBA and All-NBA defense squads.

– Hakeem is the runner-up to Charles Barkley for the NBA Most Valuable Player award.

– Hakeem leads the NBA in blocked shots and finishes fourth in scoring and rebounding.

1994 – Hakeem wins the NBA MVP and Defensive Player of the Year awards.

– The Rockets beat the New York Knicks in seven games to win the NBA championship. Hakeem is named MVP for the series.

1995 – Hakeem is bothered by injuries and illness during the regular season; his Rockets finish with a disappointing record of 47–35. Hakeem is second in the league in scoring (27.8 avg.) to Shaquille O'Neal.

– Hakeem leads the Rockets to a dramatic turnaround in the playoffs. Houston sweeps the Orlando Magic in the Finals to win their second straight NBA championship. Hakeem is elected MVP of the NBA Finals for the second year in a row.

About the Author

Miles Harvey is the author of *Barry Bonds: Baseball's Complete Player.* He lives in Chicago with his kittens Honya, Junior, and Rengin.